# The
# Hedgehog and the
# Hare

# The Hedgehog and the Hare

THE BROTHERS GRIMM

adapted and illustrated by Wendy Watson

THE WORLD PUBLISHING COMPANY
CLEVELAND AND NEW YORK

for Delafield and Betsy DuBois

Published by The World Publishing Company, 2231 West 110th Street, Cleveland, Ohio 44102. Published simultaneously in Canada by Nelson, Foster & Scott Ltd. Library of Congress catalog card number: 73-82762. Text and illustrations copyright © 1969 by Wendy Watson. All rights reserved. No part of this book may be reproduced in any form without written permission from the publisher, except for brief passages included in a review appearing in a newspaper or magazine. Printed in the United States of America.

It was a Sunday morning at harvest time. The sun was shining brightly in the heavens, the east wind was blowing warmly over the stubble fields, the larks were singing in the air, the bees were buzzing among the buckwheat, the people were going in their Sunday clothes to church, and all creatures were happy; and the hedgehog was happy, too.

The hedgehog was standing at his door with his arms akimbo, enjoying the morning breezes and slowly trilling a little song to himself, which was neither better nor worse than the songs which hedgehogs are in the habit of singing on a blessed Sunday morning.

While he was thus singing half aloud to himself, it suddenly occurred to him that, while his wife was washing and drying the children, he might very well take a walk into the field and see how his turnips were coming along. (The turnips were, in fact, in a farmer's garden nearby, and the hedgehog and his family were accustomed to eat them; for which reason they looked upon them as their own.) No sooner said than done. The hedgehog shut the house door behind him, and took the path to the field.

He had not gone very far from home, and was just turning around the sloebush at the corner there, when he observed his neighbor the hare, who had gone out on business of the same kind — namely, to visit his cabbages. When the hedgehog caught sight of the

hare, he bade him a friendly good morning. But the hare, who considered himself a distinguished gentleman, and who was frightfully haughty, did not return the hedgehog's pleasant greeting.

Instead, assuming a very contemptuous manner, he said:

"How do you happen to be running about here in the field so early in the morning?"

"I am taking a walk," answered the hedgehog.

"A walk!" said the hare with a smile. "It seems to me that you should spare your legs, and leave the walking to those of us who are better suited for it."

This answer made the hedgehog furiously angry, for he can bear anything but an attack on his legs, just because they are crooked by nature.

So now the hedgehog said to the hare:

"You seem to imagine that you can do more with your legs than I with mine."

"That is just what I think," said the hare.

"That can be put to the test," said the hedgehog. "I wager that if we run a race, I will outstrip you."

"That is ridiculous! You with your short legs!"
snorted the hare. "But for my part I am willing, if
you have such a monstrous fancy for it. What shall
we wager?"

"A gold piece and a bottle of cider," said the
hedgehog.

"Done!" cried the hare. "Shake hands on it, and
then we may as well race at once."

"Wait," said the hedgehog. "There is no such
great hurry. I have not yet eaten. I will go home first
and have a little breakfast, and in half an hour I will
be back again at this place."

Then the hedgehog departed, for the hare was quite satisfied with this arrangement.

On his way home, the hedgehog thought to himself, *The hare relies on his long legs, but I will use my wits to get the better of him. He may be a great gentleman, but he is very rude, and he shall pay for what he has said.*

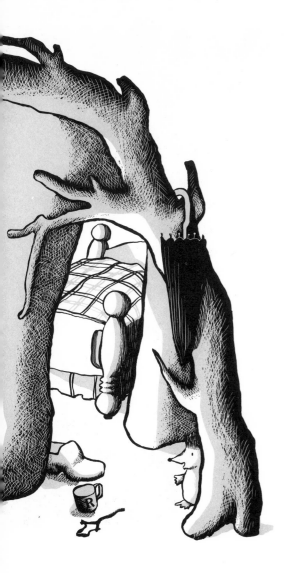

So when the hedgehog reached home, he said to his wife:

"Wife, get yourself ready quickly. You must come out into the field with me."

"What is happening?" asked his wife.

"I have made a wager with the hare, for a gold piece and a bottle of cider. I am to run a race with him, and you must be present."

"Good heavens, husband!" the wife now cried. "Are you out of your mind? Have you completely lost your wits? What can make you want to run a race with the hare?"

"Hush, woman," said the hedgehog. "I have a plan, you shall see. Get yourself ready, and come."

When they had set out on their way together, the hedgehog said to his wife:

"Now listen closely. The long field is to be our race course. The hare will run in one furrow, and I in another, and we shall begin from the top. As for your part, that is very simple."

And he explained to his wife exactly what she was to do.

When they reached the bottom of the field, the hedgehog showed his wife her place, and then walked up to the top, where the hare was waiting for him.

"Shall we start?" asked the hare.

"Certainly," said the hedgehog.

"Then both at once."

So saying, each placed himself in his own furrow. The hare counted "Once, twice, thrice, and away!" and went off like a whirlwind down the field. But the hedgehog ran only two or three paces, and then stooped down in his furrow and stayed quietly where he was.

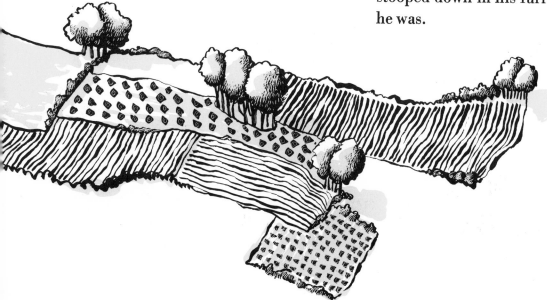

When the hare arrived in full career at the lower end of the field, the hedgehog's wife, who was waiting in her husband's furrow, met him with the cry:

"I am already here!"

The hare was shocked, and wondered not a little. He thought, of course, that it was the hedgehog himself who was calling to him, for the hedgehog's wife looked just like her husband.

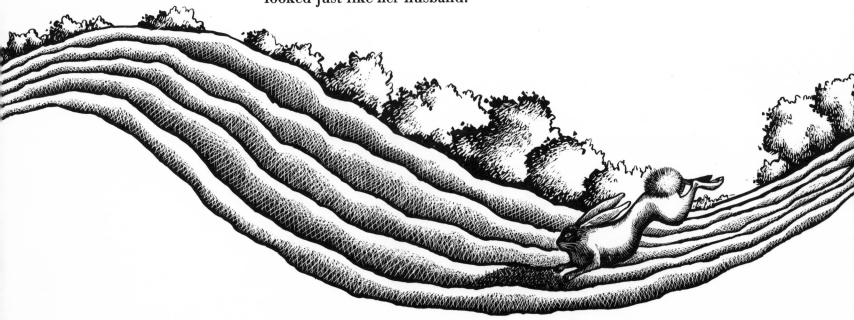

Then the hare said to himself, *That has not been done fairly,* and cried aloud:

"It must be run again, let us have it again!"

And once more he went off like the wind in a storm, so that he seemed to fly.

But the hedgehog's wife stayed quietly in her place; and when the hare reached the top of the field, the hedgehog himself called out to him:

"I am already here!"

The hare, quite beside himself with anger, cried:

"It must be run again, we must have it again!"

"Very well," answered the hedgehog. "For my part we'll run as often as you choose."

So the hare ran seventy-three more times, and the hedgehog always held out against him. At the seventy-fourth run the hare could no longer reach the end of his furrow.

"Enough!" he gasped. "Enough! I admit my defeat!" And he fell to the ground exhausted.

Then the hedgehog took the gold piece which he had won, and the bottle of cider, and called his wife out of the furrow. They both went home together in great delight, and if they are not dead, they are living there still.

*The Hedgehog and the Hare* is a fairy tale by the Brothers Grimm. The adaptation in this book is based on a translation by Margaret Hunt, who edited and translated Grimms' *Household Tales,* published by G. Bell and Sons of London in 1884.

Wendy Watson's distinctive illustrations have appeared in many books since her graduation from Bryn Mawr College in 1964. The eldest of eight children, she grew up in Putney, Vermont, and now lives in New York City where she is a full-time writer and illustrator of children's books.

*The Hedgehog and the Hare* is Wendy Watson's second picture book for World. The first, *Fisherman Lullabies,* is a collection of lullabies sung by fishermen's wives in the British Isles and New England, which Wendy Watson has selected and illustrated. The lullabies were set to music by her sister, Clyde Watson, with whom she is now collaborating on another book.

I    2    3    4    5    73    72    71    70    69